Katie Woo's

* Neighborhood *

Katie's Friends and Neighbors

by Fran Manushkin

illustrated by Laura Zarrin

PICTURE WINDOW BOOKS
a capstone imprint

Katie Woo is published by Picture Window Books,
an imprint of Capstone.
1710 Roe Crest Drive
North Mankato, Minnesota 56003
www.capstonepub.com

Text © 2021 by Fran Manushkin.
Illustrations © 2021 by Capstone.

Library of Congress Cataloging-in-Publication Data is available on
the Library of Congress website.
ISBN: 978-1-5158-8393-7 (paperback)
ISBN: 978-1-5158-9205-2 (eBook PDF)

Summary: Katie Woo's neighborhood is full of great people who make
great friends! From Mr. Kenji, who's training to be a nurse, to Miss
Bliss, the neighborhood's super-duper librarian, Katie's neighbors all
work together to make their neighborhood a wonderful place to live.

Graphic Designer: Bobbie Nuytten

Table of Contents

Katie's Neighborhood

Police

Library

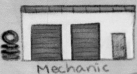

Mechanic

City Hall

Grocery Store

Post Office

School

Mr. Patel Builds

Miss Winkle told Katie's class, "Today we will learn how to build a house."

"Cool!" said Katie. "We all need a place to live."

"I have a better idea," said Roddy. "Let's learn how to wreck a house. BASH! SMASH! CRASH!"

"Wrecking a house is

too easy," said Miss Winkle.

"Building a house is hard."

Miss Winkle asked the class,

"Can you name some kinds of

houses that people live in?"

"Igloos!" said Katie.

"Yurts!" said JoJo.

"Tepees!" yelled Pedro.

"Treehouses,"
said Barry.
"I have one
in my yard."

"Those are good answers!"
said Miss Winkle. "Today, most
of our houses are made of
bricks or wood."

"My dad is a builder," said Peter Patel. "He wants us to watch him build a house."

Miss Winkle smiled. "It's a special house," she said.

"I wonder why," said Katie.

The next day the class went
to see the house. Mr. Patel said,
"First we dug a hole with a
machine called a digger."

"Then a truck filled the hole with concrete. That is the foundation."

"Right!" said Peter Patel. "It makes the house strong."

"Then it was time for
the carpenters to work," said
Mr. Patel. "They did a great
job putting up the wood."

Katie watched workers
putting shingles on the roof.

"These will keep out the
rain," said Katie. "I hate a
leaky roof."

"This is a terrible house!"
yelled Roddy. "There are no
toilets!"

"Don't be silly," said Peter.

"They are coming. My dad

never forgets anything."

"I hope they paint the walls

pink and blue," said JoJo.

"Those colors are cheerful."

"Black is better," joked

Pedro. "You can't see the dirt!"

"I want blue in the bedroom," said Miss Winkle. "And yellow in the kitchen."

"That sounds terrific," said Katie. "But the person who lives here will decide."

"Guess what?" said Miss Winkle. "I am that person! Mr. Patel is building this house for me."

"Wow!" said Katie. "Lucky you!"

"I'd like to see your house when it's finished," said JoJo. "With toilets and everything!" yelled Roddy.

"You will all see it!" said Miss Winkle. "I'm inviting the class to my housewarming party."

"Wowzee!" yelled Katie.

A few weeks later, the house was ready. It was bright and cozy.

Katie and Pedro and JoJo gave Miss Winkle flowers.

Miss Winkle smiled even more when Mr. Patel and Peter gave her a cake.

What did the cake say?

"WELCOME HOME!"

Super-Duper
Librarian

It was a cold, rainy Saturday. Katie called her friends Pedro and JoJo. They weren't home.

She wondered, "What can I do today?"

"Let's go to the library,"
said Katie's dad. "I need a new
mystery."

"And I want a funny book,"
said Katie's mom.

"I'm bringing back lots of books," said Katie. "I've read every book in the library."

"Not yet!" Her mom smiled. "Miss Bliss will find you more. She's a wonderful librarian."

On the way to the library, Katie said, "I wonder where Pedro and JoJo went today. Maybe they went to the movies."

No! They were at the library.

JoJo said, "This place is

great on a rainy day."

Pedro said, "It's great on

any day."

Katie saw many friends

from school. Miss Bliss was

busy checking books in . . .

. . . and checking books out.

Haley O'Hara and her five brothers and sisters came running in. They wanted a zillion books!

"Follow me," said Miss Bliss.

She found them books

about dragons and dinosaurs

and underwear!

Miss Bliss gave them riddle books and pop-up books and pigeon books.

Haley O'Hara yelled, "Yay, Miss Bliss!"

Katie's teacher, Miss Winkle, wanted a book about training her puppy.

"Have fun!" said Miss Bliss.

Katie told JoJo, "I want a wonderful, fabulous, super-duper book!"

"Me too!" said JoJo. "*Lots* of super-duper books."

"Yikes!" Katie shouted. "This book is about boogers!"

"Wow!" JoJo giggled. "You can find anything in a book!"

Roddy was a loud reader.

"SMASH! BASH! CRASH!"

His book was about racing cars.

"Miss Bliss found this for me," he said. "She is SO cool!"

Soon the library was about

to close. Katie felt sad.

"There is no super-duper

book for me."

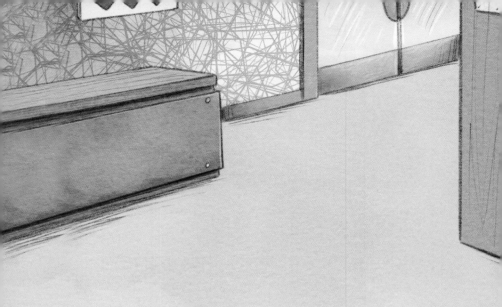

"Wait!" said Miss Bliss.

"I've saved books for you.

I found a spooky mystery!

And here's a book from your

favorite series, Betsy-Tacy."

"SUPER-DUPER!" said Katie.

Katie added a book about a
lady explorer.

Her dad said, "You read so
many kinds of books. You are
already an explorer!"

Katie and her mom and
dad hurried home.

Katie read

before supper.

She read

after supper.

She even

took her

books to bed!

When Katie fell asleep, she had super-duper dreams. They all had happy endings!

Nurse Kenji Rules!

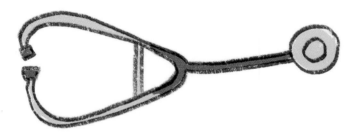

Katie had a new neighbor.

His name was Mr. Kenji. He

loved his garden, and he loved

taking photos of his family.

One day, Mr. Kenji looked worried. He told Katie's mom, "I want to be a nurse, and my final test is next week. I hope I pass it!"

"We can help," said Katie.

"Let's pretend that I am sick.

You can be my nurse. Mom and

Dad will decide if you are doing

a good job!"

Mr. Kenji came into their
house. He washed his hands.
Then he asked Katie, "What's
wrong? Why did you call me?"

Katie made a sad face. "I am feeling sick. Everything hurts."

"I'm sorry to hear that," said Mr. Kenji. "I will try to help you."

"First, I will take your
temperature," said Mr. Kenji.
He looked at his thermometer.
"You do not have a fever.
That's good!"

"But my heart is beating very fast!" said Katie "Maybe you should check it."

"I always do that," said Mr. Kenji.

"I will use this stethoscope," said Mr. Kenji.

"Wow!" said Katie. "That's a big word."

"It has to do a big job," said Mr. Kenji. "Your heart is very important."

"Your heart sounds fine," said Mr. Kenji. "It's not beating too fast."

"Can I listen?" asked Katie. "Oh my!" Katie smiled. "My heart is awesome."

Katie asked Mr. Kenji, "Can I listen to *your* heart?"

She heard: *Poom POOM! Poom POOM! Poom POOM!*

Katie's mom listened too. She said. "It is beating very fast."

"I think you are still worried about your test," said Katie's mom. "Let me make you a cup of tea. Drinking tea always makes me feel calmer."

Katie's mom poured the tea.
Oops! She spilled hot water on
her hand.

"*Ouch!*" she yelled. "It hurts."

"I can help you," said

Mr. Kenji. He washed her

hand in cool water. He put

on ointment and a bandage.

"Now it will heal."

"Thank you!" said Katie's

mom.

Suddenly, Katie's dad lay down on the couch.

"Something is wrong," he gasped. "I can't breathe! My throat and my chest hurt."

Mr. Kenji stayed calm. He took Mr. Woo's temperature. He checked his throat and his chest and his heart.

"Nothing is wrong," he said. "You are fine!"

"That's right! I am!"
Mr. Woo jumped up. "I
wanted to see if you were
calm in a crisis. You passed!"

Katie laughed. "Wow, Dad! You are great at playing pretend."

Mr. Kenji smiled too. "This practice was great! I feel better about taking my test."

Two weeks later, Mr. Kenji

took his test. He stayed calm

and smart.

He got a terrific grade. Oh, was he happy!

He told Katie and her mom and dad, "You helped me so much!"

Mr. Kenji had a party with his family and his friends. It was a great celebration. Everyone felt terrific!

Firefighter Kayla

Katie's class was on the way to visit a fire station. JoJo's Aunt Kayla worked there. She was a firefighter.

Katie told JoJo, "I can't wait to meet her!"

Aunt Kayla welcomed the class. She asked them right away, "Do your homes have smoke detectors?"

"Yes!" yelled everyone.

"Great!" said Aunt Kayla.

Then Aunt Kayla asked them, "What is the first thing to do if there is a fire?"

"That's easy," said Katie. "I would call 911."

"Not yet," said Aunt Kayla.
"First you should get out of the
house. Then you call 911."

"Oh, right!" said Katie.

"Very right," agreed JoJo.

Katie said, "Can I ask you a question?"

"I'll answer questions later," said Aunt Kayla. "First, I want to tell you about my job."

They walked around the
fire station. Pedro said, "I don't
see a pole to slide down. That
would be fun!"

"Our fire station has only
one floor," said Aunt Kayla.
"We don't need a pole. But we
have a fire dog. Flash is
a lot of fun!"

"Now I'll show you my
gear," said Aunt Kayla. She
put on her coat and her helmet
and her good, strong boots.

Katie told JoJo, "Your aunt
looks so cool!"

"My coat is heavy," said
Aunt Kayla. "It protects me
from heat and flames."

"Good!" said Katie. "Can I
ask my question now?"

"Soon," said Aunt Kayla.
"First, I'll show you my fire
truck. The siren is very loud! It
tells cars to get out of the way.
We need to reach the fire fast!"

"Our truck has tall ladders and long hoses. We go up the ladders and shoot water at the fire."

"*Whoooooosh!*" said Katie and JoJo.

"Now can I ask my question?" said Katie.

"Yes!" Aunt Kayla nodded. "Now is the perfect time."

Katie said softly, "I am worried about you. Isn't it scary to fight fires?"

"It is," said Aunt Kayla. "But we are good at doing our job. We have trained for a long time."

"Kayla and all the firefighters are a team," said JoJo. "They watch out for each other."

"Good!" Katie smiled.

Miss Winkle told Aunt

Kayla, "Thank you for letting

us visit your fire station."

All the kids cheered!

JoJo and Katie and Pedro
walked home with Aunt Kayla.
She asked them, "Would you
like to try on my gear?"

"For sure!" said Katie.

Aunt Kayla took a photo of
JoJo in her coat, Pedro in her
boots, and Katie in her helmet.
They felt very cool!

The next day, Katie and JoJo heard a fire siren. They ran out to the porch.

Aunt Kayla's truck was speeding by!

JoJo said, "I'm so proud of my aunt. When I grow up I want to be as brave as her."

"Let's be brave together," said Katie. "We'll be a team."

They shook on it!

More About Builders

Where they work: on work sites where new houses, other buildings, or new additions are being built

What they do: Builders build new buildings or sections of buildings out of materials such as wood and bricks.

What they wear: Builders wear comfortable clothes that are made out of strong, durable materials.

More About Librarians

Where they work: at schools or public libraries

What they do: Librarians help readers find books and other information. They order books and plan events for the library too.

What they wear: Librarians often wear dress clothes that look nice and are comfortable.

More About Nurses

Where they work: at clinics, hospitals, nursing homes, and schools

What they do: Nurses take care of sick patients. They also help doctors at check-up appointments.

What they wear: Most nurses wear uniforms called scrubs, consisting of pants and a shirt.

More About Firefighters

Where they work: at fire stations, on fire trucks, and at the sites of fires or accidents

What they do: Firefighters fight fires, teach about fire safety, and help at crash sites.

What they wear: Firefighters wear special pants, coats, boots, helmets, and masks.

About the Author

Fran Manushkin is the author of Katie Woo, the highly acclaimed, fan-favorite early reader series, as well as the popular Pedro series. Her other books include *Happy in Our Skin*, *Baby, Come Out!*, and the best-selling board books *Big Girl Panties* and *Big Boy Underpants*. There is a real Katie Woo: Fran's great-niece, who doesn't get into trouble like the Katie in the books. Fran lives in New York City, three blocks from Central Park, where she can often be found bird-watching and daydreaming. She writes at her dining room table, without the help of her two naughty cats, Chaim and Goldy.

About the Illustrator

Laura Zarrin spent her early childhood in the St. Louis, Missouri, area. There she explored creeks, woods, and attic closets, climbed trees, and dug for artifacts in the backyard, all in preparation for her future career as an archaeologist. She never became one, however, because she realized she's much happier drawing in the comfort of her own home while watching TV. When she was twelve, her family moved to the Silicon Valley in California, where she still lives with her very logical husband and teen sons, and their illogical dog, Cody.